Martha A Smith

Poems

Martha A Smith

Poems

ISBN/EAN: 9783742812452

Manufactured in Europe, USA, Canada, Australia, Japa

Cover: Foto ©Andreas Hilbeck / pixelio.de

Manufactured and distributed by brebook publishing software
(www.brebook.com)

Martha A Smith

Poems

POEMS.

BY

MARTHA A

THOMAS P. PEABODY, PRINTER, 52 FOURTH AVENUE, NEW YORK.

CONTENTS.

TO MY FRIENDS.

With my love this little book
I dedicate to thee:
When on its page you look,
Then you may think of me.

POEMS.

A MOTHER'S LAMENT.

When I look upon my darling,
    Whose face shines from the wall,
Sad thoughts come stealing o'er me,
    For I lov'd him best of all.

I thought he lov'd his mother,—
    How could I be deceived?
I feel my heart is breaking,
    I am so deeply griev'd.

Oh, do not think, my darling.
    Your mother loves you less,
Because that when she sees you,
She can't that love express.

A sudden pain comes o'er me,
    That racks my heart and brain;
And then I ask my Saviour
    To make it right again.

POEMS.

My joys on earth have vanish'd,—
   Every hope in life has fled;
I am only calmly waiting
   To be number'd with the dead.

Then leave me to my sorrow,
   Till grief and troubles o'er,
I'll soon be safely landed
   On yon bright heavenly shore.

I oft hear Eddie calling
   In the stillness of the night;
I know my angel baby
   Will bear me from your sight.

And father, too, is waiting,
   And beckons me away;
I soon will be in heaven,
   In that bright world to stay.

A brother, too, is watching,
   To welcome me above;
Oh, who would not dwell forever
   In that atmosphere of love?

A mother now in heaven,
   Awaiting there for me;
I am longing for the angels
   To waft my soul to thee.

If you in years hereafter,
  When mother's gone to rest,
Should feel the dart so poignant
  You thrust in mother's breast,—

Go, then, and bow to Jesus;
  He will your heart relieve;
And if you'll only trust Him,
  Your soul He will receive.

BEAUTIFUL SUNLIGHT.

Beautiful sunlight,
  Thou hast gone to appear
With thy Father in heaven,
  Where all is now clear.
We on earth weeping,
  And longing for rest;
Yours is secured
  In heaven, we trust.

Beautiful sunlight,
  We lov'd you while here.
Too lovely for earth,
  God wanted you near;

Has taken you to keep
    Free from all harm.
In His beautiful home
    Nothing more can alarm.

Beautiful sunlight.
    Oh, could you return.
And tell of those beauties
    We so wish to learn ;
God's great book is sealed
    Until we depart;
Our records are in heaven,
    May we gain the good part.

Beautiful sunlight,
    As we bid you farewell,
You to go heavenward,
    We earthly to dwell,
Till our mission is ended,
    We call'd up above,
To dwell in our Father's
    Everlasting love.

Beautiful sunlight,
    God wanted a flower;
Has taken you to bloom
    In His heavenly bower;

Transplanted above,
  One more shining light,
Making heaven, if possible,
  More beautifully bright.

Beautiful sunlight,
  God oped your seal'd eyes,
That you might see clearly
  Beyond the bright skies.
The shadow of God
  A mantle o'erthrew,
Then the beauties of heaven
  Were reveal'd unto you.

Beautiful sunlight,
  Asleep in your God,
Your glorified spirit,
  Where angels have trod.
Farewell, our dear sunlight,
  Shining above,
In the light of our Father's
  Most heavenly love.

SADNESS.

Bear with me kindly—
  Speak to me gently,—
Ere long this deep sea of grief
  Will have pass'd o'er;
And I shall go from you,
  A weary, lone pilgrim,
From this world of strife free,
  On Eternity's shore.

Alone and forsaken,
  God only my beacon,
In this gloomy hour
  Of my greatest distress,
I'll brave the dark billows—
  Let seas roll between us,
But bear with me kindly
  When beyond thy caress.

As God is my helper
  In this deep affliction,
Which has dried up my life-blood
  And sear'd my poor brain.—
Left nought in this dark world
  To see or to wish for;
Oh, stop my sad heart
  In its pulse-beat of pain.

The last blow is stricken,—
  I bow with submission;
All that soul ever struggled with
  I have pass'd o'er;
Yet my God will sustain me,
  And bear me on bravely,
Until I have pass'd through
  To Eternity's shore.

O'er the dark water
  I'll take my departure,
And flee for sweet rest
  To a quiet retreat.
Thou'lt not forget mother,
  Who did so adore thee,
Too late! no kind love
  Will her ever more greet.

Bear with me kindly,—
  I love thee so truly;
My heart weeping tears of blood
  O'er my dark way.
I'll think of thee sweetly—
  Remember thee kindly,—
Till gone to my Saviour,
  For thee ever will pray.

But when I have left thee,
  Some kind recollection
Of thy mother will come
  In deep silence of night,
In dreams o'er thy pillow,
  And gently caress thee,
As when a dear little one,
  So loving and bright,

That I've press'd to my bosom
  In fondest affection,
And cherish'd with loving
  And tender delight,
Not dreaming dark clouds
  Would ever o'ershadow
Our pathway, and leave us
  In darkness and blight.

Yet in the dim distance
  The shadow is breaking;
A beacon-light beams
  Above the bright sky,
That is leading me onward,
  With faith in my Saviour,
He soon will receive me
  In heaven on high.

Then bear with me gently—
　Speak to me kindly,—
Those that I've cherish'd
　Are dear to my heart;
Ere my life's ended,
　On thy love I depended,
Oh, speak to me kindly
　Ere from earth I depart.

CHRISTMAS MORNING.

1879.

This lonely feeling of isolation
　Creeps like the icy hand of Death
Around me,—leaving desolation,
　Chilling soul and breaking health.

I can not brighten, by my staying
　In this sad, unhappy home,
One single life by my remaining,
　Then let me fly, and be alone.

He who knoweth the sorrowful anguish
　Of this aching, lonely heart,
Will bear me onward, help to banish,
　When I tear myself apart.

This vain world is fleeting, surely.
  I feel it so, as days pass o'er;
And I know I'm fading slowly
  Into the vast Forevermore.

Yet no sad'ning thoughts steal ever,
  Nor do I bewail the call,
When I bid farewell forever,
  And laid within my narrow wall.

Thoughts of death ne'er cause a shiver,
  That once so used to chill my frame.
I only pray that God deliver
  Me from this fearful mortal pain.

This living sorrow without ending,
  Crushing life,—no hope remain,—
Is far more fearful to the living
  Than death; for then we know no pain.

Ere the damps of death close o'er us,—
  Cradled in our narrow bed,—
With cold hands clasp'd across the bosom,
  Heartaches gone when we are dead.

Let us strive, ere this last parting,
  To right all wrongs ere yet too late,
By securing to our darlings
  Equal shares in our estate.

Don't you see the shadow ever
Deep'ning to a darker day,
Unless we burst these clouds asunder,
And let them find a sunny ray?

All bright children of our being,
Loving us as well they do,—
Can you not see it is a duty
I am trying to impress on you?

Only a little while here longer
Either you or I can stay:
Try from this dark Christmas morning,
To cheer their lives from this dark day.

A MOTHER'S SORROW.

"Have you no welcome for me, mamma?"
Came in accents soft and sweet,
Trembling from the dear one's lips
As home she came to greet.

Oh, could she know the pain of heart
Her mother had endured,—
That tender cord once torn apart
Can never be restored.

To a heart that's dead unto the core
  Warm love can ne'er return;
The light put out for ever more
  Again will never burn.

The flower blooms not if torn apart,
  No germ from it can shoot;
Joy ne'er returns unto the heart,
  When dead unto its root.

And now, my darling, ere we part,
  With earnest, heartfelt prayer,
Ask God this agony of heart
  May not leave us in despair.

"Have you no welcome for me, mamma?"
  Came in accents sweet and low,
From the lips of one I've prayed so for,
  Since she from me did go,—

That ere the close of this mortal strife
  God would again restore
To my perishing, lonely, freezing life,
  Love like this once more.

"Have you no welcome for me, mamma?"
  Oh, could you but search the heart,
Or know the bitter tears I've shed,
    Since last we two did part.

A mother's love dieth not, my child,
  Although her heart may break.
All will be right in Heaven above,
  When our spirits there awake.

"Have you no welcome for me, mamma?"
  Goes ringing through the heart,
That will ne'er warm with love again,
  Until from earth we part.

I've nothing left to wish for now
  But a little spot of ground,
And a welcome to my home above,
  Where joy and love abound.

"Have you no welcome for me, mamma?"
  I replied with a broken heart—
Take what is left of a blighted life,
  Ere from earth we part.

This fleeting life hath lost its charm,
  And hearts so sorely riven,
Will ne'er know peace and love again
  Until they rest in Heaven.

CLING TOGETHER.

Cling together, you and I,—
Death will part us by and by:
'Tis not well that bitter strife
Should darken all the joys of life.

Cling together; while we stay
Let us for each other pray
All the griefs that rend the heart
From us forever may depart.

Cling together; then from home
We shall never wish to roam,
To find in other lands a rest,
United here we'll be so blest.

Cling together; soon we'll pass
Unto another life, alas!
Then let true love illume our way,
And cheer our hearts on each dark day.

Cling together; life is short.
Heart's true love can ne'er be bought.
'Tis a jewel bright and rare,—
Shining gold can not compare.

Cling together; let us try
To live true lives as years roll by.
Let not this short and weary life
Be ever spent in bitter strife.

Cling together; we'll ask of God,
Ere we sleep beneath the sod;
None but He can heal our grief,—
Only God can bring relief.

Cling together while we live,—
So that God to us may give
A peaceful life until we flee
To a happier home in eternity.

Cling together; hearts with love
Will unite in heaven above:
For this we hope—for this we pray,
To meet again at the Great Day.

Cling together, though dark shadows
  Lower around our pathway here;
There may be a brighter morrow
  And every cloud shall disappear.

Cling together; we'll hope on ever
  That true love's sun may shine again;
Ere our ties on earth we sever
  Let each the other's love regain.

Cling together; God our Father
    Will watch o'er us while we stay;
If we trust our loving Saviour,
    He will light our darken'd way.

Cling together, ere we vanish;
    One by one life's joys decay;
Those we love and fondly cherish—
    They should be so dear each day.

Cling together; God who keepeth
    Us in His everlasting care,
Will not leave, but ever loveth
    Us in this dark and drear despair.

Cling together; we'll hope on ever
    That love's sun may shine again;
Ere we leave this world forever
    Let love be ours while we remain.

Cling together; lift the sorrow
    Darkening round our pathway here;
There may be a brighter morrow,
    As heavenly hope is drawing near.

Cling together; lift the shadow,—
    Let it be our earnest prayer
That God may bring a brighter morrow
    Ere we're lost in dark despair.

Cling together; let love forever
  Unite us here, though short our stay.
Without true love our lives are ever
  A dreary and a darken'd day.

Cling together; each a mission
  God doth give us to perform.
We'll bow to Him in meek submission,
  And ask release from this dark storm.

Cling together; perhaps to-morrow
  All dark clouds will disappear.
'Mid this load of heartfelt sorrow
  We may see our way more clear.

Cling together; God's mysteries never
  Can we solve while here we stay;
But when we pass from earth forever,
  All in Heaven will be bright as day.

THOUGHTS ON MY MOTHER.

I am trying to be patient,
  And lift my heart above,
That God may still sustain me,
  And fill my soul with love,—

That I may bear my burthen,
  And feel it's for the best:
Perhaps some day the angels
  Will take me home to rest.

I oft times feel so weary,
  And then I bow my head,
And ask, " How long, my Saviour,
  Ere I'm number'd with the dead?"

Oh, mother, dearest mother,
  The tears that I have shed,
Would make a little fountain,
  Since you've lain in your cold bed.

I do so miss you, mother;
  You were my joy and love;
Now you have gone and left me,
  To rest in Heaven above.

I try to live so meekly,
  And strive to bear my cross,
While I am journeying onward,
  And on life's billows toss.

Each day my sorrows deepen,
  While struggling to be free:
I sometimes cry in anguish—
  "Oh, mother, come to me!"

And yet no lov'd voice answers,
   Still I know she hears my cry;
For I oft times feel more happy
   When I know her spirit's nigh.

But all my tears, dear mother,
   And all my prayers for thee,
Can never bring you back again
   To this sad home and me.

My heart's o'erwhelm'd with sorrow,
   And ever longs for thee,
But I know thy spirit hovers
   With loving care o'er me.

THE BRIDE'S FAREWELL.

Farewell, mother, though I leave you,
   Oft for you my heart will sigh;
And I know you love me dearly,
   Yet sadly I must say good-bye.

Farewell, father; thou didst bless me,
   Ere my lips thy name could tell;
Well I know I have thy blessing,
   Though I with another dwell.

Farewell, sisters; thou'lt remember
  Shady nooks we lov'd so well;
Where we roam'd the fields all over,
  There in fondest love we dwell.

Farewell, kind and gentle brother;
  In this hour of gentle bliss,
My heart o'erflows with love's emotion,
  While I give the parting kiss.

Farewell, friends; now we are parting,
  Your kind wishes cheer my way;
O'er my heart a deep, sweet sadness,
  Steals the memory of this day.

Saddening thoughts now swell my bosom,
  While for all I breathe a sigh;
Father, mother, sisters, brother,
  Each and all a fond good-bye.

THE BRIDAL DAY.

The bridal day!   Ah, who can tell
The hopes and fears their bosoms swell?
The fair young bride by warrior's side,
So glorious in her maiden pride.

The bridal day I'll ne'er forget
Until my sun on earth has set.
From lowering clouds and sky o'ercast
The sun is breaking through at last.

The bridal day! Oh, may each life
Be free from care and earthly strife.
May wedded life now just begun,
Be clear and bright as the rising sun.

The bridal day! As years roll round,
Oh, for you may true joys abound;
And when this fleeting life is past,
May you re-unite in Heaven at last.

ON PARTING.

'Tis over!—this great struggle.
    It has rent my heart in twain;
And I am freed forever
    From one I will not name.

Our God will judge between us
    When we have pass'd away:
I leave you to your conscience,
    Till the great judgment-day.

He who knoweth every secret—
   Every joy and every sigh—
Will bear me on my journey,
   And receive me when I die.

There is no anger in my heart
   While bidding you farewell:
I only know 'tis better
   To go from you to dwell.

Such feeling of deep hatred
   Lies rooted in your heart,
Which seems to me so earnest,
   I must from you depart.

If you think of me hereafter
   In the silence of the night,
You then will do me justice,
   For you'll know that I am right.

The still small voice of conscience
   Will ever whisper in your ear,
And warn you to be careful
   Of those I hold most dear.

I trust in my Redeemer
   For a record of my life,
When I appear before Him,
   Freed from this world of strife.

Then I leave you to your Saviour,
    While we go our lonely way,—
Trusting in the great hereafter
    Where all is bright as day.

Farewell! Still I forgive you;
    And while on earth I'll pray
That you'll be receiv'd in Heaven
    At the resurrection-day.

THOUGHTS ON DEATH.

"God moves in a mysterious way,
    His wonders to perform."
He sent a meek-eyed stranger
    To shield me from the storm.

She asked me, oh, so kindly,
    Had I made my peace with God,—
Was I ready for the summons,
    And to sleep beneath the sod.

She said the Lord had sent her
    That mission to perform,—
To prepare me for His coming,
    And to shield me from the storm.

I replied that I was ready,
    If the trumpet sound that day:
I was ready and so anxious
    From earth to pass away.

My darling little children
    And kind friends the only tie
Would hold me to the present life
    If death were drawing nigh.

Some with heartfelt sorrow
    Will regret with many a sigh,
When they see me passing over,
    And know that I must die.

My heavenly Father, give me strength,
    Is my most earnest prayer;
Oh, waft my soul to Heaven above,—
    May I Thy glories share.

I never for a moment doubt
    The goodness of my God:
That He would guide me onward,
    And lift the chastening rod.

When earthly joys all vanish,
    We see our way more clear:
Then we look into the future
    As we find death drawing near.

Death has for me no terrors;
　　I long for coming day.
This world to me is dreary,
　　My life is fading fast away.

I trust that He'll receive me
　　At Heaven's golden gate:
I'll await on earth His bidding.
　　Whate'er may be my fate.

When life becomes so cheerless,
　　Without one ray of light,
And know we're drifting onward,
　　Unto the darker night.

But a voice is whispering ever—
　　"Press onward, stricken heart!
There's rest for you in Heaven,
　　From every grief you'll part."

That kind and gentle stranger
　　Who would prepare the way,—
May I meet her in Heaven
　　At no far distant day.

EVERLASTING WOE.

Lift the shadow, oh, my God!
I bow beneath thy chastening rod!
Remove from my poor aching brain
The troubl'd thought and racking pain
I stop and shudder when I think
I'm verging on the fearful brink
　　　Of everlasting woe.

With sadden'd heart alone I go,
That those I love may never know
Their unkind words have hurt me so.
And when beyond their sight and care
My every thought and fervent prayer
Will be that God those children spare
　　　From everlasting woe.

For He alone can judge the heart,
And may they gain that better part:
No unkind thought within them dwell
When I shall say the sad farewell!
I'd rather brave the wintry blast
Than feel my soul would sink at last
　　　To everlasting woe.

With blinding tears and heart oppress'd
I go I know not where to rest!
Those cruel words, with withering blight,
Have sunk my soul in darkest night!
I pray to God that He will spare
And save me from this dark despair,
   And everlasting woe.

ADIEU, MY NATIVE LAND.

Adieu, my native land! Farewell!
 I'll sail o'er the stormy sea!
And when in a distant land I dwell,
 You may, perhaps, remember me.

I've lived to see each hope depart,
 And one by one life's joys decay:
Friends once so dear unto my heart
 Are not the same to me to-day.

No cruel wrong will e'er dissever,—
 A mother's love will ne'er depart,
But lives with life, and clings forever
 To every fiber of the heart.

Almighty God, who keepeth ever
    Us in His everlasting care,
Will not forsake us, and will never
    Leave us in dark and drear despair.

Let memory on the dreary past
    Some kindly thoughts bestow;
And o'er unkindness at the last
    A friendly mantle throw.

For I would flee forever,
    O'er land and stormy sea,
To a happy home, where never
    Unkind words could come to me.

But thee I will ever fondly love,
    Till at my Saviour's call
I go unto my home above,
    Where God keeps watch o'er all.

Time may pass till life is fled,
    And years go rolling round,
Ere we rest in our narrow bed,
    Beneath the clay-cold ground.

God may afflict whom He may love;
    Let us meekly bear the cross,
Until we're called to our home above,
    Then we'll not feel life's loss.

We long for a place of peaceful rest,
   Free from every sorrow and care:
In Heaven we may be with the blest,
   If we can only enter there.

For our heavenly home we're sighing,
   And struggling on in pain;
And with all our hearts we're trying
   Our Saviour's love to gain.

Then let us banish sorrow,
   And flee from every care;
There may be a brighter morrow,
   Then let us not despair.

For darkening clouds may lower,
   And deepen into darker night;
And every hope may perish,
   And leave our hearts in blight.

A mother is surely fading,
   And passing fast away
Unto that bright Hereafter
   Where is everlasting day.

To loved ones I will bid good-bye,
   And on my lone journey go:
Kind love to you until I die
   Is the best gift I can bestow.

And now the farewell is spoken :
  With tears and a heartfelt sigh,
I leave this parting token—
  My love and a fond good-bye.

SWEET ANNA.

Sweet, black-eyed, gentle Anna,
  I will love you all my life;
And in years that are to follow,
  You will be somebody's wife.

Near and dear to me forever,
  You are twin'd around my heart.
I will cherish thy memory ever,
  Until we from this earth depart.

We can not look into the future,
  And know the love in store for thee;
But I trust a bright hereafter,
  And many happy years you'll see.

For thee oft my prayers are wafted
  Up to God in heaven above,
That He keep thee pure and holy,
  Fill thy heart with trust and love.

Bear up bravely, show him calmly
    You can be as proud as he:
For his love you did not ask it,—
    'Twas himself untrue to thee.

Yet it grieves me one I loved so
    Should have caused a pang to thee:
Gentle, loving, kind, and truthful,
    You should ever happy be.

I trust I'll live on, gentle Anna,
    To see you yet a blushing bride:
True hearts to love and caress you,—
    A devoted husband by your side.

My sweet and gentle Anna,
    There is sorrow on thy brow.
Throw it off!—the sun to-morrow
    Will shine just as bright as now.

In years that are to follow,
    You may yet so happy be;
And I trust forget thy sorrow,
    And kindly think of me.

FRIENDSHIP'S OFFERING.

I love thee, my friend, with the truest
　　affection;
Thy sympathy falls like a balm o'er the
　　heart;
Thy friendship is lovely; thy kind dis-
　　position
Will brighten my life till from earth I
　　depart.

Oh, could I have met thee in happier
　　moments,
When this earth was so glorious,—too
　　beauteous to last;
And this life was an Eden of loveliest
　　promise;
Now gone from me forever! Farewell to
　　the past!

And left me in sadness and darkness to
　　linger,
Tlll call'd to my Maker not far o'er the
　　way;
Trusting ere my life's ended a light will
　　yet glimmer,
And brighten forever into beautiful day.

I have esteem'd thee so highly since the
    hour I first met thee,
The light of affection ever shone from
    thine eye;
With trusting devotion may it ever con-
    tinue,
Till called from this earth, and we say the
    good-bye.

Adieu, my sweet friend! As our friendship
    is blended,
May it brighten and beautify our lives
    here below!
When our lives shall be ended He on whom
    we depended—
Our Saviour will welcome us when to
    Heaven we go.

DO I LOVE THEE?

Do I love thee? Go and ask the flowers
If they love the sweet, refreshing showers.

Do I love thee? Dost thou recall the time
When first pressed to thy heart as thine?

Do I love thee? Forget not the first kiss,
When we thought our love was bliss.

Do I love thee? Can we ever forget,
Until our sun on earth has set?

Do I love thee? Tongue can never tell
How much I love thee, or how well.

Do I love thee? Would you have me say
My heart is thine till my dying day?

Do I love thee? Oft in silent thought
Thy image to my mind is brought.

Do I love thee? Yes, as the miser his gold,
Who hugs it closely, yet counts it untold.

Do I love thee? Coldness rends the heart,
And takes from love its better part.

Do I love thee? True love cannot be bought;
My feelings are too deeply wrought.

I will ever truly love thee, and thy love I'll
    ne'er resign;
While life may last my purest love shall be
    forever thine.

THE HEART'S AFFECTION.

Oh, do not chill the heart's affection;
 Crush it not, but let it bloom
And blossom ever, lest dejection
 Upon us fall and bring us gloom.

Guard the heart, and do not wonder;
 Love, though buried in disguise,
If once rudely torn asunder,   •
 Sadly, slowly, but surely dies.

The freshness of the heart is buried;
 Lost and gone is love's young dream;
The beauty of the being perish'd,
 With nought of joy doth life e'er teem.

Moving on in lone deep sadness,
 Life's trials will with us remain;
While on this earth no more of gladness
 Will brighten life; but leave us pain.

Chills the heart-pulse beating ever;
 Earthly hope forever fled;
Life's sun will now soon set forever,
 And we lie sleeping with the dead.

Oh, then, guard this tender feeling,
  Ere 'tis lost in darkest gloom;
When the fond heart is love revealing,
  Oh, send it not to early doom.

Oft from thoughtlessness of feeling
  Many a cherish'd loved one's idol
Passes from us where no weeping
  Fills the heart ne'er given in bridal.

There to meet,—await the coming
  Of the cherish'd love forbidden;
Hearts will answer those so loving
  If not on earth will unite in Heaven.

THEE, MY FRIEND.

Thy little acts of kindness
  Have won for thee a place
In my heart's pure affection,
  That time can ne'er efface.

Until I pass forever
  Unto my home above,
Memory will linger ever
  Around thy deeds of love.

In gentle accents tender,
   Kindly words and true,—
An ever friendly welcome
   I have received from you.

Now let me thank thee kindly:
   Believe me thy true friend;
On my friendship trusting ever,
   You may through life depend.

If best wishes for thee ever
   Could thy days prolong,
While on this earth forever
   This would be my song—

God spare and lead thee gently
   Unto the living Truth;
Keep thee pure and holy,—
   Guide thee in thy youth

Unto that everlasting life
   Were all is peace and love.
Free from care and earthly strife,
   To dwell with God above.

And when you this brief life resign,
   And on earth no longer stay.
In Heaven may your record shine
   As clear and bright as day.

MUSINGS.

I have thought my past life over,
   And look which way I may,
I can not see before me
   The slightest dawn of day.

Always to live thus lonely,
   Without one ray of light,
And know I'm going deeper
   Into the darker night.

Yet a voice is whispering ever—
   "Press onward, stricken heart!
There's rest for you in Heaven,
   When from this world you part."

Life can not be all sunshine;
   Take the bitter with the sweet;
The joys of the Hereafter
   We can not here repeat.

Perhaps 'tis well to suffer;
   'Tis well for us to wait
Until we meet in Heaven
   At the golden gate.

NO, NEVER MORE!

Farewell!—we are parted now!—
On thy heart and on thy brow
Is a shadow dark as night,
Which doth all my being blight:
We may meet on earth no more.
            No, never more!

'Tis with grief I am amazed,—
We coldly on each other gazed:
While dark shadows deepen o'er,
We our lives must now deplore,
And may meet on earth no more.
            No, never more!

Many a year may yet pass by
Ere we're called from earth, and die.
Then lift the sorrow from the heart
Ere we from this world depart:
We may meet on earth no more.
            No, never more!

Each to go our separate way,—
No more to meet till judgment-day,—
When, all grief and suffering o'er,
No more our lives on earth deplore:
We may meet on earth no more.
   No, never more.

Farewell, then!—a fond adieu!—
If I meet no more with you,
There's a home in Heaven above
Will not shut out those whom we love,
Where I may rest for ever more.
   Yes, ever more!

'Tis with grief and heartfelt sigh
That I say the sad good-bye.
When we live our lives apart
The tear-drops oft for thee will start:
We may meet on earth no more.
   No, never more!

LIGHT AND DARKNESS.

Light and Darkness, as I have heard say,
Lived together for many a day,
In a lovely cot near the Great South Bay.

Light was the elder by many a year;
But Darkness to Light was yet very dear.

It happened to Light to meet and to love
One now gone to his home in Heaven above.

Ere Darkness met him he was Light's lover;
After their marriage Light's kind brother.

Light wished them joy with an aching heart;
For Darkness had gained her better part.

Time passed on, and blessings were given—
Innocent children, their souls in Heaven.

"Suffer little children to come unto me,"
God said, and called them—one, two, three.

Those dear little angels lent for a while,
To cheer their hearts, to please and beguile.

Then a few more fleeting years roll'd round
Of luxury and wealth in which they abound.

Death then called upon Darkness to spare
Her love—my love;—we are equal there.

A few more years again passed by,
The idol of her heart was called to die.

How shall I describe that maiden fair,
With love-lit eyes and auburn hair?

With soul so lofty, her angelic face
Ever shone forth with heavenly grace.

The memory of that sweet girl's life
Oft cheers my heart in this world of strife.

In the first blush of youth God called away
This blooming flower with Him to stay.

Under this blow did Darkness quiver,
Beneath the rod of God the giver.

For conscience sake we hope she spent
Some time in prayer, and did repent.

Light often thought it made no impression,
Darkness had not yet learned her lesson.

Darkness soon went on a trip of pleasure,
With plenty of means and a son at leisure.

Light met them on eve of their departure
Across the seas to friends o'er the water.

Ere the farewell between them was ended,
Some talk about their mother was blended.

Their mother was left to Light's kind care,
For Darkness would not her pleasure spare.

That trust was ever held sacred by Light,
Who ever attended by day and by night,

Faithful remained to death's dark portal,
Leaving Light forever a sad lonely mortal.

Darkness returned to the land of her birth,
And found her mother no longer on earth.

Her true feelings may be stated in brief,
Remarking to Light that "it was a relief."

Light patiently waited for Darkness' return,
Their mother's affairs from her to learn.

Light then might settle their mother's estate,
And for Darkness' return did anxiously wait.

Sad was her heart, but Light will not forget
Her sisterly love and her heartfelt regret.

But Darkness declined to settle or pay
The expenses incurred while she was away.

Sad was the blow, and crushing the blight,
So to Darkness I now will wish a good night.

MY BIRTHDAY.

I've lived to see another birthday,
And would here on these pages say
A few kind words in a pleasant way
                    From mother.

That you'll not forget, as years roll round,
When hope and love with you abound,
While sleeping 'neath a grassy mound,
                    Thy mother.

In one little corner of thy heart
Let memory ever hold a part
Of kind and gentle, tender thought
                    Of mother.

Oft in hours of silent thought,
Love for thee no money bought
Exalts and thrills the loving heart
              Of mother.

Then when this world recedes from view,
And I have said the last adieu,
May nought but love then dwell in you
              For mother.

I would not have you sadly weep
When I am lying in death's sleep,
There my own true vigils keep,
              Thy mother.

Let tender thoughts of love arise
When I am gone beyond the skies,
There still may live in other eyes
              Thy mother.

Another birthday should I ne'er see,
Remember this all given to thee,
And ever kindly think of me,
              Thy mother.

With cold hands folded o'er the breast,
And passed away to peaceful rest
One that oft has fondly thee caress'd,
            . Thy mother.

When you shall say your last good-bye,
You'll think of me when called to die,
Who oft for you has breathed a sigh,
      Thy mother.

Farewell, my darlings, one and all,
I pray no harm may you befall
Until you come, at God's last call,
      To mother.

ALONE AND SO WEARY.

Alone and so weary I pine for sweet rest;
To my bosom my youngest so fondly I've
    press'd;
Apart from this world I have one tender
    heart
That loveth so fondly oft makes the tears
    start.

Dear Mattie, my darling, when this brief
    life is past,
Loving angels will bear thee to heaven at
    last.
Remember, my darling, when I'm called to
    rest
From this world-weary struggle, that I loved
    you the best. .

For you have never, darling, caused mother
    heart pain;
And I trust that in beauty and love you'll
    remain.
You have been my heart's comfort on many
    a day,
When so earnestly to God my sad heart
    would pray—

That grief so heart-rending might from me
    depart;
The wrongs heaped upon me were breaking
    my heart.
When thou, dearest comforter, to my lone
    heart I press'd,
Like a wounded dove nestling so close to
    my breast.

Sweet Mattie, my darling, a kind blessing
    given,
So greatly thou hast smooth'd my pathway
    to heaven.
Though deep griefs oppress me and sorrows
    may rend,
On thy loving affection I could ever de-
    pend.

My darling, I love thee with all my true
    heart;
Dear to memory ever till from earth I
    depart.
There my loving spirit will watch thee from
    above;
Will guard thee so tenderly till I clasp thee
    with love.

Farewell, my dear loved ones, when gone
    to my God,
Do not forget mother resting beneath the
    cold sod.

ALONE THE HEART SPEAKETH.

Alone the heart speaketh the answer to God.
Ever the heart grieveth till under the sod.
There is rest for the weary in heaven above.
Where God will receive us with eternal love.

Gladly I'd flee were this mortal life o'er,
To the realms of bliss on eternity's shore.
Alone and so weary the most hopeless strife
To lighten the burthens of this mortal life.

But all of life's trials and heart-stricken woe
Souls fit for heaven, where I trust I may go.
I'm earnestly striving, and looking above
To God to sustain me with heavenly love.

But when I am resting beneath the cold sod,
Think of me kindly when gone to my God
To be finally judged, but conscience clear,
Unto my God I will go without fear.

I have laughed with the happy, and tried
    to be gay:
All without avail, for grief hangs o'er the
    way.
Deep heart-rending sorrow, like a funeral
    pall,
Till the darkness of death casts a mantle
    o'er all.

NIGHT THOUGHTS.

Dear Mattie, my darling, ere I'm called to
    depart,
Let me once more express the deep love of
    my heart.
Your love is so constant to me day by day,
O'er my sad life it sheds a beneficent ray.

Though others may wound with piercing
　　keen dart,
Your love pours a balm o'er the wounds of
　　the heart.
In the lone hours of the night I awake with
　　the smart,—
Tears flow from my eyes from the grief of
　　my heart.

Then I arise from my bed and think my
　　life o'er,
And write to my darlings ere on earth I'm
　　no more,
That dear ones may read long after I de-
　　part,
I love and forgive them though broken my
　　heart.

In years that will follow, when little ones
　　are press'd,
If God should give them on her bosom to
　　rest,
Should they cause thee sorrow, fill thy heart
　　with grief,
And find nothing on earth can bring thee
　　relief,—

Thou may'st think of me then; just kneel
  to thy God,
Ask Him to lift from thee the chastening
  rod,
Fill thy heart with purity, kindness, and
  love,
That our spirits may mingle in Heaven
  above.

PASSING AWAY.

Passing away! Yes, gone forever more
To that never-ending beautiful shore;
With angels to welcome us with kind love,
And dwell in our heavenly home far above.

Passing away! But new beauties we find
To beckon to heaven, and make us resign'd.
Suffering and sorrow on earth are now past,
Eternity awaits us, with sweet rest at last.

Passing away into bright beaming day,
With light everlasting to brighten the way,
Triumphant faith and pureness of heart
Redeem at last when from earth we depart.

Passing away! Why here should we stay
Another world brightens with eternal day:
Lighting the pathway beaming and bright,
And leading us onward to eternal light.

Passing away! Why linger we here,
Amid all earth's trials with nothing to cheer,
And live dreary lives till at our God's call
Death at last throws a kind mantle o'er all.

TO BROTHER ALBERT.

Do not lightly cast aside
　　This simple little rhyme;
But read it over carefully,
　　When you have a little time.

'Tis written you so earnestly,—
　　Best wishes of my heart;
I would to you, if possible,
　　Some little good impart.

Brother, my only brother,
　　A temper you must confess:
Old Satan, how he troubleth,
　　And robs us of our rest.

If any wrong you then forgive,
  Like our Saviour on the cross:
You'll feel happier while you live,
  And in death will feel no loss.

Short, at best, is this weary life,
  We soon will go to rest;
Then let us do away with strife,
  And we'll be forever blest.

Throw aside all unkind feeling,
  'Twill only cause you pain;
And will not help you ever
  The better life to gain.

I think of you quite often,
  In sadness and in grief;
And pray God that He will soften
  And bring thy heart relief.

I feel you are worthy, brother,
  Of a happier life while here;
Your heartfelt love for mother
  Oft draws the silent tear.

When mourning in our sadness,
  For our lost mother dear,
Let us hope on in gladness,
  That we may with her appear.

Don't you think our mother
  Is watching us with love?
That God may bring us, brother,
  To a heavenly home above.

A kind adieu, my brother;
  If on earth we no more meet,
I trust we'll unite in Heaven,
  And there our mother greet.

Welcomed by our heavenly Father,
  When this struggling life is past;
Eternal rest in the Hereafter,
  Beautiful Heaven awaits at last.

TO MINTIE.

Thy kind voice was often whispering
  "Grandma, what can I do for you?"
Don't you think our God was listening,
  And that He will reward you, too?

Mother's sickness, groans, and moanings,
  Nearly rent our hearts in two;
Mintie's kind voice oft was asking
  "Grandma, what can I do for you?"

Oft thy kind hand, soft and soothing,
  Wiped the damps of death away,
With affection, kind and loving,
  For thy grandmother, dead to-day.

Forever this deathbed recollection
  Will rush unbidden to our view:
A place to test the heart's affection,—
  One stood by her kind and true.

Sweet girl, thy love so true and tender,
  For thy grandmother now at rest;
Such true affection I'll remember,
  Till I myself sleep with the blest.

Asleep in God, unto life everlasting
  Her tried spirit passed away;
We trust with her Maker resting,
  Until we meet at the last day.

HEART SORROW.

I will love thee, yes, forever;
  Even though we are apart,
And coldly treat thy mother,
  For you're dear unto her heart.

Yes, nestled there so fondly,—'
  On my bosom hush'd to sleep;
I've prayed to God so earnestly,
  My precious babe to keep.

Sad thoughts are ever stealing,
  When I think of other days,
When a darling little baby,
  I so loved thy cunning ways.

And oft when thee caressing,
  I thought whenever you grew
To manhood, if you'd be as loving
  As mother was to you.

But sadly thou art forgetting,
  As years go rolling by,
Thy mother's heart is breaking,
  But I'll try to hush the cry

That is welling up forever,
  And fills my heart with pain.
Then ever love thy mother,
  While she may on earth remain.

Though sadly I am weeping,
  This grief I so deplore:
Soon will I lie sleeping,—
  Yes, gone forever more.

TO SISTER SARAH.

I love to muse at the old hillside,
Where oft we've sported in girlish pride,
With brothers and sisters all so gay,
Have whiled the weary hours away.

Alas, how soon those blissful hours
Have passed away like drooping flowers!
And our dear mother from earth has gone:
Come back. dear sister, we want you home.

A sister's tears oft flow for thee,
Whene'er I pray on bended knee,—
My fervent prayers are wafted above
To greet our mother with filial love.

Ah me! the weary days pass by;
No news from the spirit-world on high;
While I am left dejected and lone.
Come back, dear sister, we want you home.

I feel the loss of our mother dear;
This world to me is sad and drear,
For earthly love is heartless and cold;
'Tis bought and sold with silver and gold.

'Tis not such love my heart would crave;
But a mother's love now cold in the grave.
My sister, I'm ever longing for thee!
Come back, dear sister, from over the sea.

TO WILLIE.

Willie, may thy life abound
    In every choicest pleasure;
And ever may thy heart be found
    True to thy loving mother.

Ever keep her memory near,
    Wherever you may wander;
You'll never find one so dear
    As thy own loving mother.

·Never grieve her tender heart:
    It may not be much longer
Ere you're call'd upon to part
    With thy own loving mother.

Love her truly ere life's fled,
    That no regret may linger
When within her clay-cold bed
    At last shall rest thy mother.

Then when the eve of life declines,
   And thou art called away,
May thy light there brightly shine,
   In spirit-love with mother.

Dear Willie, ere I bid adieu,
   I trust that you'll remember
The one who penn'd these lines to you,
   Thy own true loving mother.

TO ANNA.

Farewell, Anna, from my home
   You will pass unto another:
May you never too far roam
   From thy own dear mother.

Ever keep her memory dear,
   Wherever you may wander,—
O'er hill or dale, no one so near
   As thy own gentle mother.

When griefs oppress or sorrows rend,
   You'll find no one so tender,
And truly loving till life may end,
   As thy own dearest mother.

Even though you dwell apart,
　Remembrance lingers ever
Around the heart till you depart
　To meet thy darling mother.

One short year has pass'd away,
　And yet it seems much longer,
Since you parted one sad day
　In Ireland from thy mother.

Thy far-off home is ne'er forgot,
　Thy heart o'erflows—no wonder—
To those you left on that lov'd spot
　In Ireland with thy mother.

Oft as months and years roll round
　Thy tears for home will linger,—
Bedim thine eyes till heart rebound
　With love for thy dear mother.

And when thy journey's safely o'er,
　Thou anchored safe in harbor,
You'll be so happy ever more,—
　Welcomed by thy dear mother.

If while upon the surging sea,
　Crossing o'er the deep water,
A passing thought you give to me,
　Pray to God thy Heavenly Father.

PASSING AWAY.

Cold winter now is passing
   Away with all its gloom;
Spring days will soon be coming,
   With flowers in all their bloom.

Oh, could my sad heart brighten
   With the birds and lovely flowers
That come to us to lighten
   And cheer our lonely hours.

While dreaming on in sadness,
   With heart so grieved and lone,
I will never more know gladness
   Till I reach my heavenly home.

But flowers in all their brightness,
   And birds in all their glee,
Can never more bring lightness
   Of heart and joy to me.

Some hearts will grieve with sorrow
   When I am called away,
But the dawning of the morrow
   Will bring everlasting day.

This world is sad and dreary
  Till our struggling lives are past;
But all who are sad and weary
  May find joy and rest at last.

LITTLE BIRDIE.

Little birdie, warbling sweetly,
  As thou flittest from tree to tree,
Echoing forth thy song so lovely,—
  Beautiful birdie, I envy thee.

At my window I sit lonely,
  Listening to thy carol sweet;
Beauteous birdie, I would gladly
  Burst my bondage and thee meet.

And fly away where never sorrow
  Could cause me e'er again to weep;
But happy song, both day and morrow,
  Ever follow till we sleep.

Little birdie, warbling ever,
  In thy home upon the tree,
It will comfort me forever,
  To listen to sweet song from thee.

LONGING FOR REST.

Oh, had I the wings of a dove,
   I would fly forever away,
Where neither sorrow nor love
   Could brighten or dim the way.

Could I burst this bondage and flee
   To yon heavenly home above;
'Tis so distressing to me
   Forever to live without love.

This life is too short to live
   In continual family jar;
Better let each of us strive
   To never let anything mar.

Our pleasures and griefs here below
   Too briefly and quickly have fled;
We should enjoy life as we go,
   For soon we shall lie with the dead.

When eternity opes to our view
   May our record be bright and clear;
Oh, then let us our lives renew,
   And go to our God without fear.

For a heavenly life above
We are hoping forever to win.
If we strive with patience and love,
Surely our Saviour will let us in.

Then let us in peace depart
To a far more genial home.
In Heaven there'll be no heavy heart,
No sorrows there to mourn.

To that beautiful world of love
Oh, may we be wafted afar;
Away in the bright Heaven above
May we find the door ajar.

Then when God shall call us away
To a spiritual life of love,
Oh, may we there unite some day
In beautiful Heaven above.

At last freed from all earthly strife,
And in Heaven with the blest,
We'll not lament our present life,
When with God forever at rest.

LINES TO A FRIEND.

Dear friend, I love thee truly;
  Ever may thy life abound
In every choicest blessing
  On this earth to be found.

Then, friend, now and ever,
  While I pen these lines to thee,
Thou wilt forget me never,
  But oft remember me.

And when I lie sleeping,
  Hands clasped across my breast,
My heart no longer weeping,
  Having found its quiet rest.

You'll read with eyes o'erflowing,
  Tears from thy gentle eye
Will flow like rain in summer,
  Breaking 'neath the darkened sky.

But soon the cloud will vanish,
  And joy to you'll appear;
For you helped a soul in anguish,
  When all was dark and drear.

By soothing words endearing
  To a heart so sorely riven,
You seem to me appearing
  An angel sent from Heaven

To waft my spirit gently
  Unto that beautiful land,
Where God in all His glory
  And our loving Saviour stand.

I will love thee, friend, forever;
  May our friendship many a day
Brighten and shed ever
  O'er our lives a pleasant ray

Of sunshine to brighten ever
  Our pathway through this gloom,
Leading to sweet home hereafter,
  And rest beyond the tomb.

Then when the eve of life shall come,
  And from earth we pass away,
Unto that beautiful land beyond,
  Where forever is light of day.

This life is but a passing dream
  Of joys and sorrows given,
Where we see but the faintest gleam
  Of our beautiful home in Heaven.

PROVIDENCE.

"God moves in a mysterious way."
  We give thanks to Him and wonder
Why sin here should have such sway
  When God is over yonder.

This life is short, and God has taught
  On Him we should rely;
If through love sin has been brought,
  He will punish by and by.

Beware, ere the avenging hand of God
  Shall cause thy heart to quake:
Repent, ere with the chastening rod
  God doth His vengeance take.

Repair the wrong ere yet too late,
  Ere conscience may be stricken;
For fear you fall from high estate,
  And can never enter Heaven.

I wonder sinners go their way,
  And on earth should so prosper.
The devil with them has full sway,
  To grab them up hereafter.

Be sure thy sin will find thee out;
  Great sorrow will be thy portion;
Oh, turn thy heart, then, right about,
  To thy true one's devotion.

Let all false syrens go, through life;
  Love thine own, who, so forbearing,
Tender and true has clung through strife,
  Though oft for thee despairing.

Remember you may bruise the heart
  You once did fondly cherish;
But never till life shall depart
  Will true love ever perish.

HERE AND HEREAFTER.

When every hope on earth has perish'd,
  And every joy in life has fled,
We rest our hope on God our Saviour,
  Till sweetly sleeping with the dead.

With cold hands folded o'er the bosom,
  The silent voice no more to speak,
The soul has passed unto its Maker,
  Its record there alone to seek.

TO WILLIE.

Willie, may thy life be pure,
　In years as you grow older,
And ever may thy love endure
　For thy loving mother.

Ever keep her memory dear,
　Wherever you may wander;
In after years none will appear
　So loving as thy mother.

When griefs oppress or sorrows rend,
　There's none so true and tender,
So loving, fond, unto life's end,
　As thy own loving mother.

Never grieve her tender heart,
　It may not be much longer
Ere you're called upon to part
　With thy loving mother.

Love her truly ere life's fled,
　That no regret may linger
Around thy heart when with the dead
　Shall sleep thy loving mother.

May thy young life ever abound
　With joy and choicest pleasure;
Thy loving heart ever be found
　True to thy loving mother.

Then when the eve of life declines,
　And thou art called away,
May thy light there brightly shine,
　With thy loving mother.

Dear Willie, ere I bid adieu,
　I trust that you'll remember
Her who penn'd these lines to you,
　Thy own true loving mother.

—✦—

LONELY MUSINGS.

I'm sitting alone this twilight hour,
　While thinking of the past.
Once was mine a beautiful bower,
　And I a merry country lass.

It reminds us of our youth again,
　When pleasure led the way;
While I so happy to remain
　In my father's cot by day.

From morn till eve the sweetest sound
  Of a happy, joyous life;
The ringing laugh ere did resound,
  Ne'er marred by bitter strife.

The twilight hours are now as bright,
  But there cometh no happy sound
To fill the heart with fond delight,
  And with true joy rebound.

God's mysteries we may never know,
  Or why he doth afflict;
We only know 'tis ever so,
  And our Father who directs.

Only for a time this strife,
  Then this brief life will be o'er;
And we shall find eternal life
  On yon bright heavenly shore.

ETERNALLY RESTING.

Eternally resting, sweetly sleeping,
  Entered the pearly gates so bright,
Sorrow ended, no more weeping,
  In thy beautiful home of light.

Thy pure spirit is wafted upward,—
Gone unto its God who gave;
Resting sweetly, we following onward
To our rest beyond the grave.

Beautiful thought!—thy life is ended;
Never more tears can dim the eye.
Thy gentle soul is forever blended
With the angels above the sky.

Although our hearts will mourn forever
For our mother called away,
We will cherish the fond hope ever
To meet again at the last day.

SHE IS NOT DEAD.

She is not dead, but sleepeth,—
Gone to God who gave;
Flowers around her bloometh,
As they laid her in the grave.

Only passed, not gone forever,
Unto her heavenly home,
To meet her loving Saviour,
And left us on earth alone.

We miss thy face so kindly,
  In thy accustomed seat;
Thy gentle voice so sweetly
  Will never more us greet.

Thy mission here is ended;
  Thy work on earth is o'er;
Thy spirit-life is blended
  With angels forever more.

TO ALIDA.

Dear Alida, thy tender mother
  Left thee for the spirit-land;
Gone unto her loving Saviour,
  There to join the heavenly band.

Dry thy tears. A dutiful daughter
  Has no cause for one regret;
If her heavenly father calls her,
  He will never thee forget.

Oft I've watched thy tender feeling
  For thy mother pass'd away.
Well I know that in God's keeping
  Leaving thee so oft I pray

God to keep thee pure and holy,
　Fill thy heart with trust and love,
Until thou anchorest safe and surely
　In thy home in Heaven above.

THE PRESENT AND THE FUTURE.

By trials and afflictions
　We see our way more clear;
Our heart's best affections
　Are often buried here.

When our earthly joys shall vanish,
　We'll hope for a future bright:
When from this life we perish,
　Heaven opens to our sight.

Beyond the smiling and the weeping,
　Where no sorrows dim the eye,
Forever a welcome greeting
　Awaits us when we die.

Oh, who would live and suffer
　In this fleeting world of pain?
Let us go unto our Saviour,—
　With Him ever to remain.

WEEP NOT FOR ME.

Weep not for me, when I am dead,
And laid within my narrow bed;
Shed not a tear o'er my lone bier,—
With the trumpet-sound I shall appear.

Weep not for me, but let me rest,
With cold hands folded o'er the breast.
Think how sweet my sleep will be,—
Prepare for death, then follow me.

Weep not for me; but pray to God
That when thou liest beneath the sod,
Thy troubles o'er and sorrows past,
That we may meet in Heaven at last.

Weep not for me; with heart oppress'd,
I've longed so much for this sweet rest.
Should sorrows ever rend thy heart,
You'll wish, like me, from earth to part.

Weep not for me, but save your tears;
You'll need them all in after years.
And many tears perhaps you'll shed
Ere you lie sleeping with the dead.

Weep not for me, nor heave a sigh:
Relieved of all my cares I die,
And pass beyond this vale of tears,
Where grief or sorrow ne'er appears.

Weep not for me; but strive to live
So that your God to you may give
A peaceful life, with happy love,
And meet at last in Heaven above.

Weep not for me; the end of life
Will end all sorrow, care, and strife.
To each and all I bid adieu,
Trusting in Heaven to meet with you.

Weep not for me; my spirit love
Will wait for you in Heaven above,
Until the trumpet-sound is given,
When we'll again unite in Heaven.

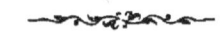

PREPARE TO MEET THY GOD.

"Prepare to meet thy God!" is sounding
    In my ears from morn till night.
I well know my heart is longing
    With heavenly spirits to unite.

Who would wish on earth to linger,
　When every joy in life has fled?
Left to live and suffer ever,
　Till resting with the sleeping dead.

As we find this world receding,
　The beauty of Heaven doth unfold
Unto our vision, ever leading
　Beyond this earth to joys untold.

Oft our hearts may weep in sorrow,
　And deep regret; but still we pass,
Here to-day, but where to-morrow?
　Our earthly life is fleeting fast.

We go unto the unknown future,
　Far away and out of sight;
The soul shall ever with its Maker
　In endless joy at last unite.

We pass unto our Heavenly Father;
　Just beyond is a beautiful light
Beckoning us onward to our Saviour
　Where no more is darken'd night.

Prepare to meet thy God, forever.
　When our mortal race is run,
Let us hope that our hereafter
　May be like the rising sun.

MARRIAGE OF A YOUNG FRIEND.

Marriage, sweet girl, sends a thrill through
    my heart
Which the terrors of death could never
    impart.
You give your young life to your husband
    to keep,—
A jewel more precious than the wealth of
    the deep.

May his love be as deep as the depths of
    the ocean,—
May no sorrow e'er mar the heart's fond
    devotion;
And may you ne'er be like a ship founder'd
    at sea,
With no mate at the helm to watch over
    thee.

May your lives ever glide on in pleasure
    complete;
When from earth you depart in Heaven
    may you meet;
And then ever together in the bright world
    above,
May you be clasped in the embrace of
    eternal love.

OUR LITTLE RAYMOND.

Our baby-love is sleeping
   In his little casket-bed.
Do not grieve,— stop weeping:
   Leave him resting with the dead.

Flowers bloom around his pillow;
   Their fragrance fill his bed.
Our hearts are grieved with sorrow,
   For the dear one lying dead.

Little angels now forever,
   In their home in Heaven above;
To meet on earth again never,
   But trust in heavenly love.

Mother, thy budding flower
   God has called away
To dwell in his beautiful bower,
   Resting in Heaven to-day.

Oh, who would live forever
   In this fleeting world of sin?
Our home is waiting ever,
   And God will take us in.

The coming of the morrow
  May be our brighter day,
Then who would live in sorrow,
  When we in Heaven may stay.

By prayer and careful watching,
  Till our work on earth is o'er,
Our home above is waiting,
  When we reach the heavenly shore.

There will be friendly greetings,
  By lovely angel forms;
There our loved ones are waiting
  Beyond this world of storms.

There's balm for thy heart-sorrow
  In this lovely living trust.
Let us every comfort borrow
  Till we mingle with the dust.

Our love for children ever
  Dwells within our heart:
Mother-love can never
  Cease till we depart.

Well I know the anguish—
  The bleeding heartfelt sore—
That we can never banish
  Till at rest forever more.

Our baby-loves are sleeping
　In their little grassy bed:
Friends on earth are weeping
　For loved ones with the dead.

When our earthly mission's over,
　And we sleep beneath the sod,
In Heaven our friends discover,
　In the eternal home of God.

Little Raymond now is watching
　At the pearly gate so white,—
At Heaven's portal waiting,
　Till your spirits may unite.

Be ready for the summons
　When your Maker calls away:
There will be a glad re-union
　At the resurrection-day.

THE DEPARTED ONE.

Only one short year has passed and fled,
　Forever that sweet face of thine,
Pillowed so oft upon my breast, now dead!
　God willed it so,—why should I repine?

''Tis hard to tear my soul apart from thine,
  For I had dreamed sweet dreams of thee;
How can I lose thee and forever resign
  All in this life so dear to me.

''Tis the will of God to suffer here below;
  To love and lose all that is dear.
Then struggle on in sadness here and woe,
  To make our way to Heaven more clear.

I feel thy power when sorrow ever
  Comes to me with withering blight;
Thy remembrance leads my mind forever
  To thy heavenly home beyond my sight.

Oft in whispers thy sweet voice above
  The cooling breeze of twilight hour I feel,
And hear thy whispered vows of love,
  And fancy my arms around thee steal.

But those happy days have forever passed,
  I feel what I have loved and lost;
And long to lay me down and be at rest,
  Nor longer here upon life's billows toss'd.

This little grassy mound holds all I love;
  Oft I strew fresh flowers upon thy grave;
While thy sweet and pure spirit from above
  Will ever watch o'er my soul and save

From dark despair, and gently lead
  Your love left only a little while behind
To watch and pray, hoping some day indeed
  To mingle in beautiful spirit-love divine.

The joys and pleasures of this earthly life
  No more can fill my soul with love:
In the grave they're buried with my wife,
  Till we re-unite in Heaven above.

LITTLE ALBERT.

Little Albert, baby-love,
Blossoming in thy home above;
Filled with angels such as thee
Beautiful Heaven is supposed to be.

Hush, dear mother, hush thy weeping;
God forever thy babe is keeping;
All thy grief can ne'er restore
Thy bright cherub ever more.

Oh, so many hearts are sighing
When their baby-loves are dying;
God's mysteries never can dissever
Baby-love from thine forever.

God holds the casket in His keeping;
Sweetly thy darling baby's sleeping.

"Suffer little children to come unto me,"
Our Saviour said. He will watch over thee.

Leading thy pathway to life immortal,
Thy baby awaits thee at Heaven's portal.

Resting so sweetly in his little casket-bed,
Love and leave him with the dead.

Then when the trumpet-sound is given,
Hope to meet thy babe in Heaven.

THE DEATH OF IONE.

As I looked within the casket,
   At the lovely sleeper there,
And thought of her hereafter,
   Who did for Heaven prepare.

Her face was so angelic,
   To see her was to feel
Her pure spirit was in Heaven,
   At our Saviour's feet to kneel.

Then, mother, trust your daughter
   Will be waiting there for thee,
To welcome you to Heaven
   When from this life you're free.

I can see a light of glory
   Around her angel form,
As she welcomes you, her mother,
   From this bleak world of storm.

And father, too, and brother,
   She'll we watching for above;
Awaiting you in Heaven,
   With outstretched arms of love.

And Alice, her only sister,
   Will not be forgotten there.
If she trusts in her Redeemer,
   With heartfelt, earnest prayer.

Then do not grieve, kind mother,
   That Ione has gone before,
To wait for you in Heaven,
   On the bright, eternal shore.

Be cheerful, mother, ever,
   And happy while you may;
For you'll surely meet your darling
   At the resurrection-day.

THOUGHTS ON DEATH.

This life for me is nearly o'er,
I see beyond the shining shore,
Where I may rest forever more,
    In that bright world above.

Oh, take me home, my God, I pray.
I would not in this cold world stay,
'Tis such a dark and dreary way,
    And such bright Heaven above.

Soon I'll sleep my last long sleep,
    The sleep that knows no waking.
And pass forever from your sight,
    Like the dawn gently breaking.

And when you these lines may read,
    Think how soon that we shall be
Calmly sleeping with the dead,
    Then you perhaps will think of me.

I feel old age is creeping o'er me,
    And here I would not strive to stay;
I know my God is beckoning onward
    To prepare me for the coming day.

May your life glide peacefully onward
  Unto that everlasting day;
And you, sweet girl, meet me in Heaven,
  When from this earth we pass away.

~~~~~~~

SLEIGHING.

The bells are merrily ringing,
  There's snow upon the ground,
The sun is brightly shining,
  And all seems joy around.

I muse upon the happy time
  When I was young and gay;
Many fondly thought of me,—
  Would take me in their sleigh.

But now old age is o'er me,
  They quietly pass me by,
And seek those who are fairer,
  And younger than am I.

I could enjoy the sleighing
  As much as the young and gay;
But young folks think their elders
  Have already had their day.

With heartfelt sigh I'll stay at home.
And for the young folks pray
That they may now enjoy their lives.
For youth will soon pass away.

However, I will not murmur,
For it is the will of God
That I should feel thus lonely,
And I bow beneath His rod.

A PRAYER ON THANKSGIVING DAY.

Oh, give me strength, Father, I pray,
To see my path in this dark day!
Oh, give me wings, and let me fly
To the bright realms beyond the sky.

This earthly life is so lone and drear
That death to me would sweet appear.
I pray that God who rules on high
May take me home when I shall die.

Gladly from this world I'll flee,
Feeling a perfect trust in Thee.
Almighty ruler, God of love,
Take me home to Heaven above.

LONGING FOR REST.

Oh, Father, dear Father, look down upon
    me,
And take thy poor child up to Heaven
    with thee.
I am asking and wishing and longing for
    rest;
Dear Jesus, do take me to Thy home with
    the blest.

As I think of my life and my desolate
    home,
My thoughts go forth in deep anguish to
    roam,
I'm wishing and longing, if such it might
    be,
That I soon may be safely in Heaven with
    Thee.

The days of my youth have long since
    passed away;
Old age is coming o'er me, and what does
    it say?
To look upward and onward, and earnestly
    pray
That the troubles of this life may soon pass
    away.

LOVE, WHAT IS IT?

Love, what is it? An exquisite feeling,
  Beautiful only if a lifelong dream.
Later in life we may not possess it:
  Life is the happier as it may seem.

Love if forsaken the heart may be breaking;
  Joys if once lost we can never redeem.
Though we may strive to gain Cupid's favor,
  Forever gone from us is love's lost dream.

Love, as it should be, each one caressing,—
  True to each other, with fondest devotion,
No shadow of doubt to mar the affection,—
  Is not this ideal love's truest emotion?

Heavenly love!—oh, may we possess it,
  And go from this world to mansions above.
Earthly love can not compare with the joys
  Of our Heavenly Father's protecting love.

DEATH.

Death!—what is it? Why do we shudder
    To meet the grim monster face to face?
'Tis ever with us,—we can not escape it;
    Ere long we'll be in Death's cold embrace.

If only ready to meet the dread summons
    When God may call us to mingle with dust,
And feel our hearts pure, sins all forgiven,
    Awaiting our reward in Heaven with trust.

This subject on which we too seldom reflect,
    Hoarding up wealth to harden the heart,
Death comes at last in all his dark terrors,
    Shrieking we bid the grim monster depart.

But 'tis too late! Death's icy cold fingers
    Clasp us already tight round the heart:
Prayers nor riches will not then avail us
    In the dread hour when called to depart.

TO MY SISTER,

ON THE DEATH OF HER DAUGHTER.

Do not grieve for Gertie,
  Though she has passed away;
For she has gone to Heaven,
  With the angels there to stay.

Dear sister, trust in Jesus,
  As your Gertie did while here:
She will welcome you to Heaven
  When from earth you disappear.

Ever think of her an angel
  In that better world above,
To welcome you, her mother,
  With outstretched arms of love.

Then throw away all sadness,—
  Be cheerful while you may;
For you'll surely meet your darling
  At the resurrection-day.

SPRING.

The sun is shining,—birds are singing,—
  Everything seems bright and gay;
But to me this world is dreary,
  And I long to pass away.

Spring has come with all its brightness;
  The birds now flit from tree to tree;
Why should my heart be so lonely?
  From earth to Heaven I would flee.

With the Spring bright days are coming,
  Joys lost to me forever more:
All my hopes are now in Heaven
  To meet with loved ones gone before.

A THOUGHT.

Who can know the spirit's yearnings?
  Who can into the future see?
When our work on earth is over,
  Happy in Heaven we may be.

LIFE AND DEATH.

My weary life is almost o'er,—
  Yon bright Heaven stands in view:
No more pain, and no more sorrow,—
  Loved friends on earth I bid adieu.

Welcome death, and all beyond it:
  From this earth I long to flee.
What is life?   A living sorrow!
  What is death?   I trust in Thee.

REMEMBRANCE.

Ah, well do I remember,
  For how can I forget
One moonlight eve of summer
  When first by chance we met
On the loveliest isle that sparkles
  In our own blue native sea,—
'Tis a chain that binds me ever
  To loving thoughts of thee.

REST AT LAST.

Rest at last, your sufferings o'er;
You see beyond the shining shore
Where you may rest forever more,
    In that bright world above.

Our Saviour whom you now may see
Has given His precious life for thee;
And by your faith and trust in Him
Has taken you from this world of sin.

You're safe at home and happy there,
And did with trust for Heaven prepare:
I feel you're safely landed there,
    With perfect trust and love.

MY PRAYER.

I shrink beneath life's chilling blast,
And now, oh, God, I crave, at last,
Thy help and Thy protecting care,
Ne'er withheld when asked in prayer.
Thou who see'st the sparrow's fall,
Oh, leave me not, bereft of all.

When life became a cheerless blank,
Beneath dark and deep waves I sank,
I raised my voice with anxious cry—
Receive me, Lord, when I shall die.

When griefs oppress and sorrows rend,
Only on Thee we may depend:
My every hope and constant prayer—
God save me from my dark despair.
In Thou alone I'll put my trust
Until I mingle with the dust.

I care not what the world may say,
To Thee devoutly I will pray
That Thou wilt wash my sins away.
Ever in Thee, with fervent prayer,
I'll trust for Thy protecting care.

I pray for help from Thee above,
For still Thou art a God of love.
No taunt or wrong will ever more
Cause me again to feel heart-sore.
I'll leave this unkind world and flee
Away and shield myself in Thee.

GO, FALSE DECEIVER.

Go, false deceiver, go thy way:
We'll meet again at judgment-day.
You won my heart to throw it by,
And cause me ever more to sigh.

I believed thee ever good and true,
And gave my heart in trust to you.
I loved too well, and wrecked my life
Through thy false vows; and mortal strife
Is tearing my body and soul apart:
Gladly would I from earth depart.

Whenever you look upon my face,
Saddened forever, no joy you'll trace.
You know who caused this terrible sin,
And wrecked a life all pure within.
Alone to meet the withering blast,
My blighted life is failing fast.

Dost thou not think an avenging God
Will overtake thee, ere beneath the sod?
Then if God should vengeance take,
And make thy heart with fear to quake,
Dost thou not fear sinners such as thee
May never peace or happiness see?

And when upon their dying bed,
Be haunted by the deeds they did,
And when the damps of death close o'er,
Nor peace nor hope for ever more,
The wrath of their offended God
Will reach them e'en beneath the sod.

BURYING-GROUND MUSINGS.

Why mourn we for departed friends?
When dead life's joys and sorrows end,
If only ready to meet our God,
We need not fear being under the sod.

Thoughts while I these graves explore
Of so many loved ones gone before:
My father and mother, brother dear,
And many others resting here.

Their immortal spirits watching above
To welcome us with heavenly love
Whenever our Maker calls us home
To dwell with Him and forever to roam
The beautiful land of golden light
In Heaven above where all is bright.

Soon our mortal race is run,—
Our work on earth forever done.
The churchyard has for me a charm:
No fear have I of grief or harm.

I have prayed for death in its darkest form,
To relieve me from this world's cold storm
So cruelly beating o'er my poor head,
Till forever at rest with the sleeping dead.

Why should we in this dark world stay?
In Heaven there shines eternal day.
Oft I ask of God, in sore distress,
How long ere He will give me rest.

My sorrows all ended, I gone to my God,
I long for this quiet beneath the green sod.
Tread softly, my loved ones, over my head,
While gazing upon my calm and quiet bed.

DEAD LOVE.

It comes too late, that smile alluring;
  Too late for me the smothered sigh;
The love is dead, so long enduring,
  For one who passed me coldly by.

Too late to bridge the deep gulf over;
   Closed the floodgate to the heart;
There is a grief too deep for weeping,
   Where never more the teardrops start.

Think not the void within my heart
   Can be filled with golden treasure:
The gift of love might do a part
   To bridge this deep gulf over.

Years of agony have chilled a heart
   Love long for thee enduring.
Now rent apart no teardrops start
   O'er the grave of this lost feeling.

Sorrows turn the heart to stone,—
   Leave it bleeding, rent asunder.
Griefs that let no teardrops start
   Have left me of that number.

Memory dwells o'er the happy past:
   Oft fancy there would linger;
Heart would leap, and love repeat;
   Alas, now fled forever!

Then wonder not, for every heart
   Sooner or later may discover
It was not well to tear apart
   Love once lost is lost forever.

TO LOUISE.

Thy tender love for thy father last night
Has won my heart unto you, quite.
May he ever, sweet girl, highly prize
The love that shone in thy bright eyes.

May you ever be thus kind and true
To a father so truly devoted to you.
You'll never find on this earth below
More true a heart to love you so.

Should sorrow ever thy heart oppress,
Your father would never love you less:
Then a gentle mother's tender care
Will follow her children everywhere.

Dear girl, who, having so many to love,
Till God shall call thee home above,
Be gentle, loving, kind, and true,—
A blessing to those who are loving you.

May they long be spared in tender love.
If God should call them to rest above,
May He soften the blow to thy tender
Until you from this earth depart. [heart.

May your life be joyous, beautiful, bright,
Few clouds o'ershadow thy pathway light.
May the beauty of thy heart remain,
Until at last you heaven gain.

Farewell, dear girl: these lines by me
Are written in kindest love to thee.
Adieu, and may you happy be;
And sometimes kindly think of me.

TO ANNA ROBERTS.

Forget not, Anna, as years roll round,
    Thy kind and loving mother.
Lips can not utter a sweeter sound:
    Wilt thou ever this remember?

Mine has passed from earth away,—
    My own, my darling mother;
But I hope to meet some day,
    In spirit-love, remember.

Thou'lt not forget we're growing old,
    And ever love thy mother:
Never let thy heart grow cold,—
    'Twould grieve her, thou'lt remember.

Now that her youth has pass'd and fled,
 Ever cherish thy loving mother.
Should any unkind word be said,
 'Twould grieve her, thou'lt remember.

We all possess a tender heart,
 And fondly love our mother.
Bitter wrongs rend love apart,—
 Joy thrills the heart, remember.

When coldness chills a loving heart,
 We flee unto our mother;
Though it takes from love its better part,
 We grieve while we remember.

Beneath any crushing weight of woe,
 Those who have a loving mother
To cheer them under the cruel blow,
 She'll cling to us, remember.

Adieu, sweet Anna, fare thee well.
 Let us love and cherish mother.
Forget me not.   No pen can tell
 How much we love, remember.

TO A FRIEND.

On thy smiling face I can trace
  A beauty fresh and rare,—
That memory never can efface,—
  How shall I this declare?

I only know a beautiful rest
  Comes over this lonely heart
When I enter thy home so sweet.
  And leaves me when I depart.

Thy earthly home is lovely, friend:
  May no sorrow ever blight;
While you on our God depend,
  With loved ones you unite.

This life is but a passing dream,
  To joys and sorrows given,
Affording but the faintest gleam
  Of peace and rest in heaven.

THE LADY AT THE BALL.

REFLECTIONS AT THE GRAND UNION BALL,
SARATOGA, 1879.

Dear lady, amid the festive scenes to-night,
Thoughts come o'er me while I write:
When looking upon thee smiling with glee,
I thought thou must so happy be;
Never dreaming thy heart ached so within,
Caused by another's terrible sin.

While listening to thy tale of woe,
It touched my heart with sadness so.
This life is but a passing dream;
We smile at its follies, and happy seem;
But the aching heart God sees within;
We would live our lives all free from sin.

God afflicts those He loves, we know not why:
It will all be revealed after we die.
Oft we may weep and draw the deep sigh:
Little the world knoweth how bitter the cry
Goeth up to our God in heart-stricken woe,
While sorrows oppress as through life we go.
Our griefs will be over when this life is past,
If we are faithful our reward comes at last.

THE DEATH OF LULU.

Lulu's at rest in the arms of her Saviour,
Who said, "Suffer little children to come
unto me."
Sweet bud of bright promise resting so
sweetly
With Jesus in glorious immortality.

Transplanted to Heaven this bud of sweet
beauty
Ere blossomed on earth to a full bloom-
ing flower;
Its perfume and beauty fill the portals of
Heaven,
Around the bright throne in its beautiful
bower.

God's mysteries, mother, we may never
discover,
Till called from this earth where all is
revealed;
While resting our faith in our kind, gentle
Saviour,
Our trust in sweet Heaven forever is
sealed.

There with dear Lulu, your bright little
    cherub,
  Your spirits will mingle in Heaven's own
    light;
United forever, your light ever shining,
  And nothing obscuring your vision all
    bright.

Be happy, kind mother, though Lulu's de-
    parted;
  Never let your sweet eyes overflow with
    sad tears;
Take up the cross meekly: the crown will
    be brighter,
  When called from this earth and eternity
    appears.

A WISH.

I wish for thee, mother,
  With the kindest affection,
Long years of true happiness,
  And beautiful love,
From all the beloved ones
  That around you do mingle,
Trusting devoted affection,
  And love from above.

FAREWELL TO LIZZIE.

Farewell, Lizzie; across the ocean
  Thou hast gone a mother to greet;
Proving thus a child's devotion,
  Longing loved ones home to meet.

Wishing a safe and pleasant journey
  Across the billows o'er the sea,
Until thou anchorest safe and surely
  In old Ireland home to thee.

We miss thy faithful service ever:
  Oft remembrance brings to mind
Deeds of kindness live forever,—
  We'll ne'er another Lizzie find.

And I know a welcome greeting
  Awaits thee o'er the deep blue sea.
Warm hearts there await thy coming
  In old Ireland home to thee.

Farewell, Lizzie; may God our Saviour
  Keep thee in His tender care;
Bear thee gently to thy mother,—
  This will be our earnest prayer.

God bear thee safely on thy journey
  While upon the surging sea,
Until thou'rt anchored safe in harbor,
  In old Ireland home to thee.

LINES TO A FRIEND.

Ah, well do I remember
  When you and I first met:
It was bitter cold, and winter,
  For how can we forget?

It was bitter, bleak, and dreary;
  We were following to the grave
A dear kind friend and lovely,—
  God gave and He will save.

They laid her to rest so tenderly,
  To sleep in her cold bed,—
While weeping friends then sadly
  Left her with the quiet dead.

Only her frail body reposing
  Beneath the snow-clad ground,—
Her glorified, beautiful spirit,
  We trust her Saviour found.

EDNA CLAIR.

Edna Clair is a darling,—
　A precious little pet;
A tender flower blossoming,
　We can ne'er forget.

Edna Clair is beautiful,—
　Every one must admire.
May she ever be dutiful,
　And all that you desire.

Edna Clair is loving,
　Gentle, lovely, and true:
May she prove a blessing
　Ever, mother, to you.

Edna Clair, kind father,
　God hath given to thee:
Teach her to love her Saviour,
　That she may happy be.

Edna Clair, sweet baby,
　Grandma bids adieu.
Some day, little beauty,
　I may meet with you.

TO MY NIECE.

Around the dying bed of mother
　Oft my heart went out to thee,
With a fervent wish to Heaven
　That thou'lt ever remembered be.

Yours a love so true and tender,
　With no eye but God to see;
And I truly felt thy kindness,—
　Thou wilt ever remembered be.

Thy fond affection for grandmother
　Was so beautiful to me,—
While I thought of thee so often,—
　Thou wilt ever remembered be.

We will ne'er forget thy goodness,
　Nor will God in whom you trust:
Always be thus kind and gentle
　'Till you mingle with the dust.

I pray God to keep thee ever
　Pure and holy in His love,—
Safely anchored in His harbor,
　When you pass to Heaven above.

FRIENDSHIP.

TO A DEAR FRIEND IN HER SICKNESS.

If the friendship I bear thee
  Can brighten thy toil,
Or help thee to bear it,
  In this world of turmoil:

Though dark be the day,
  Yet a brightness may glimmer
To lighten thy way
  To bright Heaven forever.

With patient resignation,
  And trust in His love,
Thou'lt reach thy destination
  With angels above.

Although darkness may linger,
  The bright day will come,
And shine o'er thy pathway
  When life's work shall be done.

Thy toils and afflictions
  Are so gently leading,
Sayeth our Father in Heaven
  Come all ye heavy-laden.

THE OLD PEAR-TREE.

Oft I've mused in girlhood,
   Beneath the old pear-tree,
Of blissful days in the future,
   When somebody's love I'd be.

My memory often lingers
   O'er the days when I were free,
Believing joy would last forever,
   And somebody's love I'd be.

Life then was sweet and happy,—
   Oft remembrance brings a sigh:
In youth I dwelt so fondly,—
   On somebody's love I'd rely.

That dear one's love I cherish'd,
   Thought of under the tree,—
Fled years ago,—it perish'd,—
   That somebody's love for me.

Alas! I am near forgetting
   How quickly bright hours do flee.
I'm aged now, though trusting
   Yet somebody's love I'll be.

But I will e'er remember,
   There's bitter with the sweet:
With faith in the great Hereafter,—
   There my Saviour's love to meet.

IN MEMORY OF MRS. W. E. HORWILL.

Thou art gone, but not forgotten:
    An angel thou art now,—
With a harp within thy hand,
    And a crown upon thy brow.

Thou art gone, but not forgotten:
    Laid away in peaceful rest,—.
Thy cold hands folded gently
    Across thy clay-cold breast.

Thou art gone, but not forgotten:
    Thy many deeds of love
Are recorded up in heaven,
    And thou'lt reap thy reward above.

Thou art gone, but not forgotten:
    Full oft our hearts will weep.
God eternal up in heaven
    Will thee ever safely keep.

Thou art gone, but not forgotten:
    Thy pure spirit, robed in white,
Enter'd into the life immortal,
    There with angels to unite.

Thou art gone, but not forgotten:
    Gone to join the chosen band,—
At thy Father's feet now sitting,
    Crown on brow and harp in hand.

DEATH OF BERTHA SHULTZ.

Thy gentle spirit has taken flight
   To the realms of angels on high;
Fled forever from our sight,—
   Farewell, sweet Bertha, good-bye.

Child of promise,—sweetest beauty,—
   With us on earth though short thy stay,
To know thee was to love thee dearly,—
   Too soon, alas! thou pass'd away.

Cherish'd one of fond affection,
   Even though our hearts may break,
We'll bow beneath this sad affliction,
   God who gives at last will take.

Though 'tis hard to learn the lesson,
   We'll bear it meekly: if we win,
By and by the gate will open,
   To admit our souls within.

Memory throws a mantle over
   Beauteous Bertha robed in white,—
Watching at God's portal ever,
   Waiting with lov'd ones to unite.

Mother, our hearts are griev'd with sorrow,
   Over thy irreparable loss:
Here to-day, but where to-morrow?
   The reaper, Death, will claim at last.

Gone, sweet Bertha, budding flower:
  God hath call'd thee to His fold,
Transplanted safely to His bower,
  Thy sweetest beauty to unfold.

Unto thy Father's love forever,
  Farewell thou beautiful beaming light,
Although we miss thee, and shall ever,
  We say "God bless thee," darling bright.

GRANDMA'S SOLILOQUY.

There is Nellie and Lulu,
  And Eddie so sweet,—
Too lovely they are
  For my pen to repeat.

Sweet little darlings,
  Their love is so true,
With clinging devotion,
  Fond mother, to you.

While father so loving,—
  So highly doth prize,
With tender affection,
  He can now realize

The true beauty of life
  Is to cherish with love
His children and wife,
  Till God calls above.

BEAUTIFUL LIGHT.

The beautiful light heavenward
 Is no more obscured from view:
The Master is beckoning onward,—
 There is work for me to do.

I'll take up the cross and follow,
 Isolated from those I love;
Bid adieu to grief and sorrow
 Till I rest in Heaven above.

Then when my work is over,
 I'll silently glide away,
Home to a loving Saviour,
 Where all is bright as day.

LOVE THEE.

Love thee? Yes, while life doth linger,
Around our pathway blending ever,
Two hearts united, our loves are plighted,
While on earth we are united.

Coldness nor wrong can e'er dissever
My heart from thine,—'twill love forever:
Around our very life and being
Closest ties of love are twining.
Weaving there a home of beauty,
Where to love is our true duty:

Then our hearts would never wander,
Nought on earth could e'er be fonder.
For each other our loves are blended,
Until on earth our lives are ended.

This is love, with Heaven's blessing,—
Each ever true and fondly caressing,—
Until we pass from earth away,
To re-unite in Heaven at a future day.

TO BELLE.

I could not close this little book
  Without for thee some kindly feeling:
While o'er these pages you may look,
  My love for thee I am revealing.

And when I gaze upon thy face,
  And meet affection there so tender,—
A gentle loving heart I trace,
  That forever I'll remember.

My friend, thou hast within thyself
  One of God's best blessings,—
A pure heart within thy breast,—
  So loving, fond, and trusting.

Long years ago, since first we met,
  Among my friends you number,—
A dear loved one I'll ne'er forget,
  But fondly e'er remember.

ADIEU, MY FRIEND.

Adieu, my friend, the tear of sorrow
  Dims the eye, and we must weep;
For you are leaving, and to-morrow
  Will be upon the briny deep.

When the billows roar around thee,
  Fear not for thy little band:
God guides and saves upon the sea,
  As well as rules upon the land.

May God in loving mercy ever
  Abide with you upon the sea;
And conduct thee safely to the harbor,
  Where kind friends may welcome thee.

Adieu, my friend, a short time only,
  Ere you're welcomed home again
By true hearts that prize you truly,—
  Still in our friendship you'll remain.

IDA IN HEAVEN.

Oft thy beauteous saintlike face
   Shines o'er my lonely way,—
O'erwhelms my soul while I trace
   Thee a spirit in Heaven to-day.

And while I thus enraptured gaze
   On thy lovely face, I'm weeping,—
Remember'd days, and thy loving ways,
   While thou in death art sleeping.

In fancy oft I see thee yet:
   Ever thy sparkling eye of blue
Reflecting light and love upon
   The friends whom once thee knew.

And oft in fancy now I paint
   Thy many acts of love;
Thy angelic life without restraint
   Was meant for Heaven above.

Now thou hast joined the angel band,
   Though friends on earth are grieving;
With crown on brow and harp in hand,
   Thy reward in Heaven receiving.

LITTLE DAISY.

Little Daisy, transplanted above,
To bloom in the garden of heavenly love:
Too lovely for earth, God called her away,
Home with the angels forever to stay.

'Tis a beautiful thought: thy Daisy not here,
But waiting in Heaven till you may appear,
Freed from this earth and all bitter strife,
And meet your embrace in everlasting life.

Take comfort, beloved ones; your loss is
    her gain.
Gone her pure spirit in Heaven to remain.
A beautiful thought, when this life is o'er,
Lov'd ones will welcome on Heaven's bright
    shore.

Little Daisy, ere from earth passed away,
Threw up her arms to her mother to say
Receive me in heaven, our beautiful home,
Where we together with angels may roam.

So this sweet child from earth passed away,
Fled her sweet spirit with the angels to stay.
God has received her in Heaven above,
To bloom in His garden of beautiful love.

THY SPARKLING EYE.

Thy sparkling eye and soul-lit face
Shine on my heart with heavenly grace.
The beauty of thy face divine
Will live in my heart in future time.

I feel, sweet one, I could resign
All dear in life to be ever thine,—
In winter's cold or summer's heat
Could worship ever at thy feet.

The ecstasy my heart doth thrill,—
With all my soul I love thee still.
Gently thy tender love sublime
I earnestly pray may yet be mine.

Around thee all seems beauteous love,
Fitting mate for angels above.
Yet linger in this world below,
I pray thee, dear one, I love thee so.

Oh, turn those beauteous eyes on me;
Let me once more thy love-light see.
Little Cupid has touched the heart,—
I will love thee, dearest, till death us part.

THOSE BEAUTEOUS EYES.

Those beauteous speaking eyes of thine
Bespeak a soul of love divine.
Had I a dear one such as thee
I'd bow me down on bended knee
Unto my God, and thus declare
My fervent love, in earnest prayer
That He may keep thee ever true
To thy dear mother devoted to you.

Within thy home may true love abide.
And when thou art a blushing bride,
May thy husband prove kind and true,
And worthy of a prize like you.

We only need look on thy face,—
There we may true beauty trace.
Those eyes so tender and so sweet
Doth us with friendly welcome greet.

A power of love within them lie,—
The lovely tint of the azure sky.
Those sweet bright eyes of heavenly hue
Draw me, sweet girl, with love to you.

MY HAIR IS SILVERED O'ER.

My hair is silvered o'er the brow,
    And fled the beauty of the face,
Where once did blushing roses grow,
    Forever a settled sadness trace.

Oft memory lingers round the past,
    When happy-hearted, light, and free.
Believing joy and love could last,
    When thoughtless in my girlish glee.

Oh, ask me not to smile again,
    While passing through this life of woe:
Remember few could bear the pain
    I've struggled long and hard to do.

In dreary solitude I wander,
    Bereft of every hope in life
Beyond the wish to fling asunder
    All earthly ties and end the strife.

Amid the burning deeds of wrong
    I fly for rest, my God, to thee,—
To whom my hope and faith belong
    Till death shall set my spirit free.

REMEMBRANCE.

Ah, well do I remember,—
　For how can I forget
One moonlight eve of summer,
　When first by chance we met
On the loveliest isle that sparkles
　In our own blue native sea,—
'Tis a chain that binds me ever
　To loving thoughts of thee.

Ah, well do I remember,—
　For how can I forget?
Those moonlight eves of summer
　Though past, I may regret:
For we have met and parted,—
　Each to go our separate way,—
'Tis a thought that lingers ever,
　And the past recalls to-day.

Ah, well do I remember,—
　For how can I forget?
Fond memories of my girlhood
　Twine round my heartstrings yet:
And still the heart doth oft recall
　Fond thoughts of youthful days,
When love's sweet flower was budding
　Beneath its springtime rays.

Ah, well do I remember,—
  For how can I forget?
Though fled, forgotten never,
  Until life's sun doth set:
While fancy often lingers
  O'er the happy, blissful past,—
O'er the days when I so merry
  Thought joy and love would last.

Ah, well do I remember,—
  For I have ne'er forgot:
Those balmy eves of summer
  Have left a fragrant spot;
For memory often wanders,—
  In fancy again I tread
Those blissful days all over,
  And sigh that they have fled.

Ah, well do I remember,—
  For how can I forget
Those moonlight eves of summer,
  When so often I have set
Within the mellow gloaming
  Of the twilight's gentle hour,
With many a dearly loved one,
  That I'll see again no more.

Ah, well do I remember,—
　For I can ne'er forget:
Those moonlight eves of summer
　Fondly linger round me yet;
While oft the sigh I smother
　For the sweet remembered past,
And the cherished ones who loved me
　With a love too pure to last.

Ah, well do I remember,—
　For I can ne'er forget
Those moonlight eves of summer
　When many a time I've set
Within some leafy bower,
　In my girlhood's happy day,—
With loved ones all around me,
　Have whiled the hours away.

Ah, well do I remember,—
　For how can I forget
The moonlight eves of summer
　Shine just as brightly yet.
And in the far-off heavens
　Shines many a gleaming light;
Where in the great Hereafter
　Our spirits may unite.

Ah, well do I remember,—
　　For I can ne'er forget:
I would be of that number
　　Who may with angels sit.
Then the future life may brighten
　　With the dawn of coming light
That shines direct from Heaven
　　To guide us to the right.